A Tail OF TWO CHRISTMASES

Darla Purgason

WHO Chains YOU PUBLISHING

ILLUSTRATED BY APRIL PEDERSEN

Published by Who Chains You Books
P.O. Box 581
Amissville, VA 20106
WhoChainsYou.com

Written by Darla Purgason
Illustrated by April Pedersen

ISBN 13: 978-1-946044-36-5

Printed in the United States of America

First Edition

Dedicated to
All Those
Who Find
and Rescue
Animals in Need

*T*was the Eve before Christmas

And all through the condo

Not a soul was stirring,

But a kitten named Mambo.

He was prowling and meowing

And licking his fur.

He needed a present—

A gift from him to her.

"Your name can be Mambo
'Cause everyone will see,
You've got style and rhythm,
Come on, live with me."

His angel had a dog,
And the dog's name was Clancy.
They had a small place,
It was nothing that fancy.

*B*ut the two became friends,

They got along very well.

Clancy, too, had been rescued

Oh, he had stories to tell!

The angel spent weeks

Trying to pet Mambo's head;

But Mambo was afraid,

So he'd dance off instead.

"Oh Mambo, I love you,
Why can't you understand?"
But still Mambo remembered
The hurt caused by hands.

He wouldn't be held
Or cuddled so near.
The hands of a human
Were something to fear!

She bought him a bed,
Some catnip and stuff.
But when she tried to pet him,
Her hand filled with fluff.

Although he was grateful,
He still danced away.
"Maybe I'll pet you
On some other day."

$\mathcal{N}$ow here it was Christmas
And he had not a dime.
What could he give her
And still be on time?

She got him new toys;
He knew, he had peeked!
What could he give back?
He worried all week.

Clancy wasn't bothered,
As his eyes closed in bliss.
"I wake her each morning
with a big, sloppy KISS!"

Then Mambo had an idea
And it created such glee.
"I know what to give her:
I'LL GIVE HER ME!!!"

*C*hristmas morning dawned bright
As Mambo danced in.
His perfect present
Came with a grin.

She was barely awake;
she stretched and she yawned.
But the change in Mambo
On her quickly dawned.

*H*e pranced into her room,

And his tail did a twirl.

"Here's my present to you,

You lucky, LUCKY GIRL!!"

With a mighty leap,

He jumped into her arms.

"With you I am safe,

I will come to no harm."

So Mambo gave up his fears
On that fine Christmas Day.
His angel shed happy tears,
As they started to play.

He wiggled, she giggled,
And they all had such fun.
The battle for trust
Had finally been won!

"You two are the best GIFT,"
his angel happily declared.
Clancy sighed, and Mambo purred
Cherishing the love they shared.

Christmas is for giving
And Mambo was willing to bet
This Christmas morning
Was one they'd NEVER FORGET!

About the Author

Darla Purgason is retired from a career in Washington, D.C., and keeps busy with cat rescue as well as caring for her own four beloved long-haired kitties. She enjoys vegetarian cooking, books on tape, and embroidery. She is the author of **A "Tail" of Two Christmases**, and a contributing author to **More Rescue Smiles**. Darla makes her home in Culpeper, Virginia, with her husband Paul.

About the Illustrator

April Pedersen is a freelance illustrator and author based in Reno, Nevada. She is partial to frogs, snails, video poker, science fiction, geocaching, and chess. April is the author and illustrator of **Slow Moe**, and the illustrator of **A "Tail" of Two Christmases, Adopting Adele, Brave Benny, Bravo's Freedom, Happy Dog Coloring Book,** and **Courageous Conner.**

More from Who Chains You Publishing

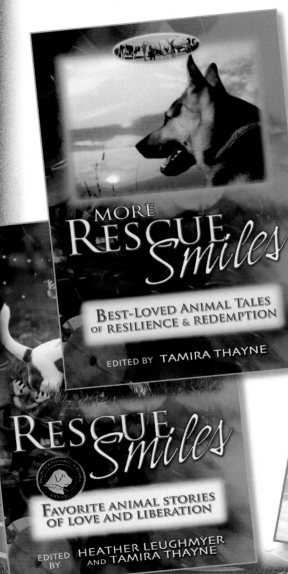

MORE
RESCUE
Smiles

BEST-LOVED ANIMAL TALES
of RESILIENCE & REDEMPTION

EDITED BY TAMIRA THAYNE

RESCUE
Smiles

FAVORITE ANIMAL STORIES
OF LOVE AND LIBERATION

EDITED
BY HEATHER LEUGHMYER
AND TAMIRA THAYNE

Happy Dog!
COLORING BOOK

ILLUSTRATED BY
April
Pedersen

WRITTEN AND
DESIGNED BY
Tamira
Thayne

Kindness to Animals
SERIES

Brave Benny

Heather Leughmyer
Illustrated by April Pedersen

About Who Chains You Books

At Who Chains You we publish books for those who believe people—and animals—deserve to be free.

Who Chains You Publishing brings you books that educate, entertain, and share gripping plights of the animals we serve and those who rescue and stand in their stead. Come choose from our many children's, young adult, fiction, and nonfiction titles. Visit us today at WhoChainsYou.com!

Made in the USA
Columbia, SC
30 October 2018